W9-AAZ-544

Rose Red & Snow White

A GRIMMS FAIRY TALE

Retold and Illustrated by

RUTH SANDERSON

Ruth Sanderson 2000

LITTLE, BROWN AND COMPANY

Boston New York Toronto London

First Edition

The text for *Rose Red and Snow White* was retold from the
Brothers Grimm.

Library of Congress Cataloging-in-Publication Data
Sanderson, Ruth.
Rose Red and Snow White : a Grimms fairy tale / retold and illustrated by Ruth
Sanderson. — 1st ed.
p. cm.
Summary: A bear, befriended by two sisters during the winter, returns one day to
reward them royally for their kindness.
ISBN 0-316-77094-9
[1. Fairy tales. 2. Folklore — Germany.] I. Grimm, Jacob, 1785–1863. II. Grimm,
Wilhelm, 1786–1859. III. Schneeweisschen und Rosenrot. English. IV. Title.
PZ8.S253Ro 1997
398.2′0943′02 — dc20
[E] 95-14518

10 9 8 7 6 5 4 3 2 1

NIL

Published simultaneously in Canada by Little, Brown &
Company (Canada) Limited

Printed in Italy

Paintings done in oil on canvas

Calligraphy by Judythe Sieck

Special thanks to Liza and Jaclyn
for being such great models

Once upon a time, a mother lived with her two daughters in a lonely cottage at the edge of a forest. Two rosebushes grew next to the front door, one with fiery red blossoms and the other bearing delicate white flowers. The two daughters were just like the roses, and their names were Rose Red and Snow White. Rose Red had bright red hair and a happy, carefree temperament. She loved to run across the fields, singing at the top of her voice. Snow White had a more gentle nature. She preferred to care for their animals, help with the housework, and read whenever she had the time.

Rose Red and Snow White walked hand in hand wherever they went, and when Rose Red said, "We will always be together," Snow White would reply, "For as long as we shall live." Though the two girls often roamed about the woods searching for berries and wild mushrooms, no wild beast ever harmed them. The rabbits and squirrels ate from their hands, the deer grazed

beside them, and even the wolf passed by with no ill intent. If the sisters stayed too late in the woods and night overtook them, they would sleep curled up on a mossy spot until morning. Their mother never feared for them when they were together.

Rose Red and Snow White helped keep their mother's cottage clean and neat. Every morning in the summer, Snow White would put a fresh bouquet of flowers next to her mother's bed before she woke. In the winter, Rose Red lit the fire and put on the iron kettle.

When the snow fell on cold winter nights, their mother would say, "Rose Red,

Snow White, come, and we shall have a story." Then they would gather close by the fire, and she would read aloud to them while the two sisters listened and sewed or spun. Sometimes a newborn lamb would lay next to them and a tame dove would perch behind them with its head tucked under its wing.

One evening as they sat by the fire, there was a banging at the door. The mother said, "Quick, Rose Red, open the door! It must be a traveler seeking shelter."

Rose Red unbarred the door and opened it. She thought she saw a man standing in the shadows. But in an instant she knew that she was wrong. For it was a bear and not a man that thrust its huge hairy head in through the door. The lamb started to bleat, the dove flew to a rafter, and Snow White hid behind her mother's chair.

Rose Red tried to close the door to prevent the beast from entering, but to the astonishment of everyone, the bear began to speak! "Do not be afraid," he said. "I will not harm you. I am half frozen and wish only to warm myself a little."

"Poor bear," said the mother. "Come and lie down by the fire. Only take care not to singe your fur." Then she said to her daughters, "Come out — the bear will not harm you. For I see he is an honest creature." Rose Red and Snow White came out from their hiding places, and even the lamb and dove drew near.

The great bear asked the girls to beat the snow out of his fur. The sisters fetched a broom and brush and swept him dry. Then the beast stretched out in front of the fire and growled contentedly. The girls soon grew quite comfortable around their huge guest, and they teased him playfully. They tugged at his ears, sat upon his back, and pretended he was a horse. Rose Red braided some of her hair ribbons into his fur. The bear good-naturedly submitted to all their fussing.

When it was bedtime, the mother said to the bear, "You are welcome to lie on the hearth, for I would not send you back out on such a cold night." The next morning, Rose Red opened the door for the bear, and he trotted out into the sunshine.

All winter long, the bear came every evening. He would listen to ther read and then lay down on the hear and let the girls play th games with him. I' growled at them, they only laughed and called him their "dear bear."

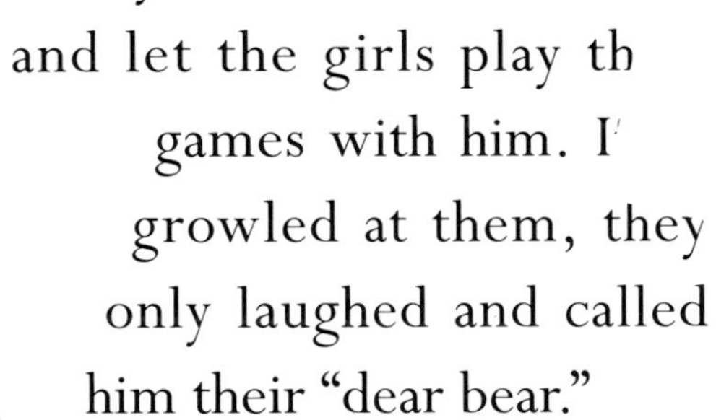

With the arrival of spring came the bear's departure. "I must go away now," he said. "And I shall not return for the whole summer."

"Where are you going, dear bear?" asked Rose Red.

"I must guard my treasure. Wicked dwarfs hide underground all winter, but now that it is warm, they will be about their mischief of spying and stealing."

Snow White and Rose Red sadly bid their friend good-bye, and Rose Red unbarred the door for him. As the bear left, a piece of his fur caught on a nail, and Rose Red thought she saw a bit of something golden glittering under his hairy coat. But the bear ran off into the woods before she could get a closer look.

A few days later, when the girls went into the woods to collect kindling, they came upon a clearing where a huge tree had fallen. They noticed a small creature jumping up and down on top of the trunk, and when they came closer, they saw it was a dwarf. The end of his long beard was stuck in a crack of the tree.

“Why are you just staring at me?” screamed the dwarf. “Can’t you help?”

“What happened?” asked Snow White.

“You dumb, inquisitive goose!” bellowed the dwarf. “I was splitting the tree in order to get a few chips of wood for the kitchen stove when my beard got caught! So here I am, you moonfaced ninnies! And don’t you dare laugh!”

The girls tried to hide their smiles as they attempted with all their strength to pull the beard out of the tree, with no success. "Fools!" yelled the dwarf. "Can't you do any better?"

"Just be patient and hold still," said Snow White, who could not bear to see another in trouble or pain. She took a pair of sewing scissors from her pocket and carefully snipped off the end of the dwarf's beard. The dwarf then jumped from the tree and grabbed a bag of gold that was hidden amongst its roots.

"Such rudeness to cut my beautiful beard!" he muttered as he swung the bag over his shoulder, and then he disappeared into the forest without a word of thanks to the two sisters.

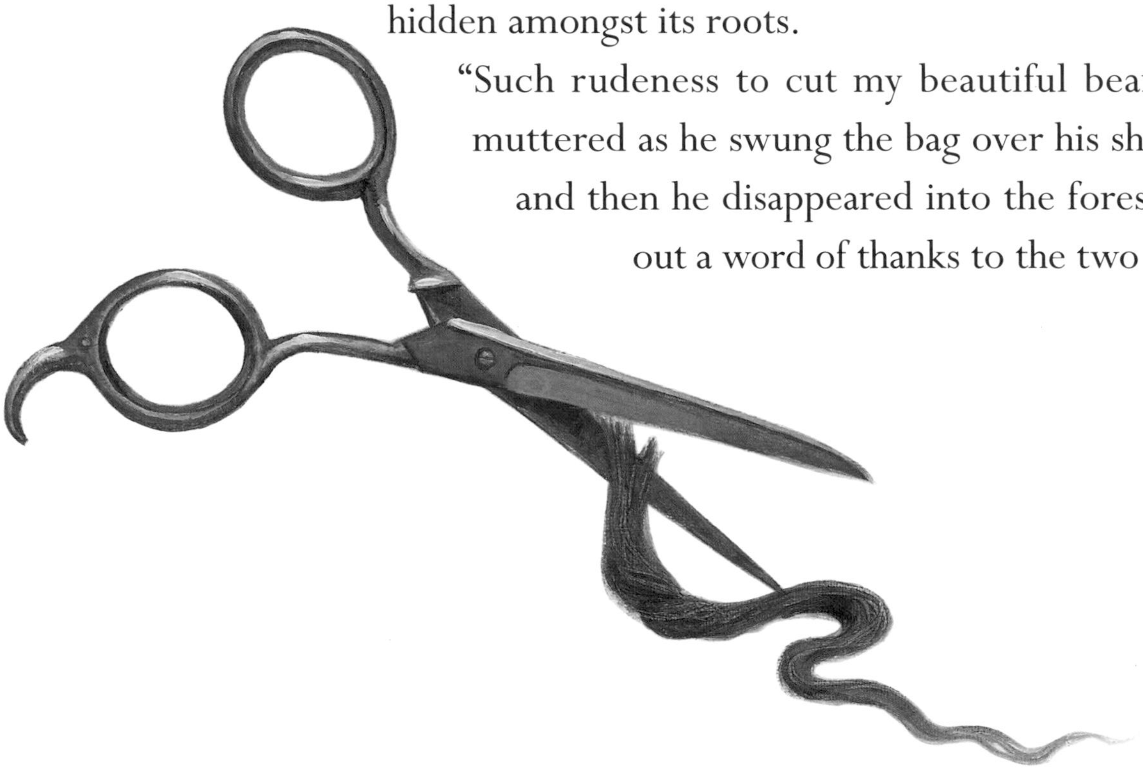

The next day, Rose Red and Snow White went to a nearby stream to catch fish for their supper. They were surprised to see their new acquaintance the dwarf hopping along the shore like an enormous grasshopper. His beard was tangled in a fishing line while a large fish pulled on the line's other end. The fish was too strong for the little man and dragged him closer and closer to the water's edge.

The sisters ran to the dwarf and held him fast, but they had no luck untangling his beard. Snow White had no choice but to cut off another small piece of it.

The dwarf flew into a rage. "You toads!" he yelled. "You have disfigured me again! My people will laugh at me, and it is all your fault!" Then he fetched a sack of pearls that had lain hidden nearby and dragged it away.

Not long after, the two sisters were on their way to town to buy some needles, thread, and ribbons. The road led through a field that was strewn with large boulders. As they walked along, they noticed an eagle circling the sky above them. The eagle descended slowly and settled upon a nearby rock. Suddenly a sharp cry pierced the air. The girls ran forward and saw the dwarf dangling from the talons of the great bird!

"Help!" he cried. The girls grabbed hold of his feet and were almost carried away as well. At last the eagle let loose his prey, and all three tumbled in a heap on the ground.

When the dwarf recovered from his fall, he began to scream at the sisters again. "Why weren't you more careful? You have torn my coat to shreds, you useless wretches!" Then he snatched a bag of precious gems from behind a nearby bush and vanished under a rock.

The sisters, who had become quite accustomed to his ill treatment, just shook their heads and continued on to town. But on their way home, they passed by the same field and surprised the dwarf as he was pouring out his bag of gems upon a flat rock. It was late in the day, and he must have thought no

one would be passing by at that hour. The gems sparkled so beautifully in the rays of the setting sun that the girls drew near to gaze at them.

"What are you gaping at?" snarled the dwarf. His face turned dark with rage.

Then the ill-tempered little man began to jump up and down, up and down. He spluttered and could not get out even a single word, so great was his anger at being discovered. He started to gather up the jewels when a ferocious growl was heard in the distance. Moments later a huge brown bear trotted out of the woods.

The dwarf leapt back in fear, but the bear was already too close for him to escape. "Oh, please, Great Bear, spare me and I will give you a big reward!" cried the dwarf. "All those precious gems will be yours if you only let me go." But the bear continued to growl deep in his throat and continued lumbering toward the cowering dwarf.

"I am thin and old, not tasty at all," whined the pitiful creature. "Here, look at those young plump girls. Surely they would be tender morsels for you! Eat them, I say, not me, for goodness' sake!" But the great bear did not heed his words and gave the dwarf a single blow with his huge paw. The dwarf fell dead in an instant.

The girls held on to each other in fright and ran toward home. But the bear called after them, "Rose Red and Snow White, don't you remember me? Do not be afraid!" Then they recognized the voice of their dear bear and stopped. Rose Red and Snow White stood quite still, for a marvelous sight appeared before them.

As the bear approached, he rose up on his hind legs and his brown furry coat slid to the ground. A dashing young man dressed all in gold stood in his place.

"I am the son of a king," he explained, "bespelled by that evil dwarf, who stole my treasure. I was forced to wander in the shape of a bear until his death freed me from the enchantment. Now he has gotten his just reward for his evil deeds."

In time, Snow White married the prince and Rose Red married his brother. Their mother lived with them happily for many years. She brought the two rosebushes with her and planted them outside her window at the castle.

They bloomed beautifully each year and bore the most fragrant red and white roses in the kingdom.